Beastly Banquet

Beastly Banquet

TASTY TREATS FOR ANIMAL APPETITES

❖•❖•❖•❖•❖•❖•❖•❖•❖•❖•❖•❖•❖

animal poems by **Peggy Munsterberg**

pictures by **Tracy Gallup**

Dial Books for Young Readers ▮ **New York**

Published by Dial Books for Young Readers
A Division of Penguin Books USA Inc.
375 Hudson Street
New York, New York 10014

Text copyright © 1997 by Peggy Munsterberg
Pictures copyright © 1997 by Tracy Gallup
All rights reserved
Typography by Amelia Lau Carling
Printed in Hong Kong
First Edition
1 3 5 7 9 10 8 6 4 2

Library of Congress Cataloging in Publication Data
Munsterberg, Peggy, date.
Beastly banquet: tasty treats for animal appetites/
animal poems by Peggy Munsterberg; pictures by Tracy Gallup.
—1st ed. p. cm.
Summary: A collection of lighthearted poems about the feeding habits
of elephants, spiders, snakes, dogs, and other animals.
ISBN 0-8037-1481-5 (trade).—ISBN 0-8037-1482-3 (library)
1. Animals—Food—Poetry. 2. Children's poetry, American.
[1. Animals—Food habits—Poetry. 2. American poetry.]
I. Gallup, Tracy, ill. II. Title.
PS3525.U62B43 1997 811'.54—dc20 94-2951 CIP AC

The full-color artwork was prepared using gouache and watercolor.
It was then color-separated and reproduced as red, blue,
yellow, and black halftones.

For Ephraim, Aryeh, and Rachel

P. M.

For my parents

T. G.

Crocodile Bird

There's a little bird
   That lives by the Nile,
And she gets her food
   From the crocodile,
For the beast likes to bask
   On the sandy shores,
And the bird hops in
   When it opens its jaws,
And there in its mouth,
   As bold as a thief,
She pecks up food
   From between its teeth!
Then out she hops,
   That bird of the Nile,
And runs to another
   Crocodile.

Robin

The Mother Robin says,
  What do you want,
  What do you want,
  O what do you want for lunch?
The little Robins cry,
  Big fat worms and juicy slugs,
  With dragonflies and lots of bugs!
  That's what we want,
  That's what we want,
  O that's what we want for lunch!

Butterfly

The butterfly
That flutters by
Sips nectar from the flowers:
A pleasant way
To spend a day
Of golden summer hours.

Blue Whale

The whale is as big as a two-ton truck,
    And he's just as fat as a blimp,
But all he eats are tiny things
    About the size of a shrimp;
Thousands and thousands every day,
    Enough to fill a boat,
Straining them out of the salt-sea brine
    And slurping them down his throat.

Spider

The spider spins an airy web—
Her dinner plate, her hammock bed—
And there she sleeps and there she eats,
And there she stores her little treats,
For the sticky web entraps the fly
That comes too close as it zigzags by:
"Aha!" says the spider, and starts to munch
On legs and crispy wings for lunch.

Goat

What funny things
   The goat tries to eat!
An old straw hat,
   A dried-up beet;
Brambles, eggshells,
   A piece of twine;
Even a sock
   Hung up on a line.
No wonder he's cross,
   If that's all he's fed!
No wonder he butts
   With his bone-hard head,
For he must be so starved,
   He's really mad,
And that's the reason
   He acts so bad.

Giraffe

She walks on stilts
Like a circus clown,
And when she eats,
She doesn't stoop down,
For her neck soars up so high,
She grazes upon
The *tops* of the trees,
Munching and crunching
The twigs and leaves,
Her head against the sky.

Bat

Behold the bat!
    He darts on high,
And eats his dinner
    In the sky;
For when it's dusk,
    The bat comes out
And wheels and swerves
    And skims about,
Gulping here,
    And gulping there,
Eating insects
    In the air.

Seagull

The hungry gulls
   That soar and wheel,
Drop down to the dump
   To look for a meal.
The food they find
   Is spoiled and smelly,
But each one eats
   To fill its belly,
For seagulls love
   What we like least:
To us, it's garbage,
   To them, a feast.

Goldfish

Fish in fishbowls always get
Food that's soaking, soppy wet,
Floating down, drifting by
Like snowflakes falling from the sky.

Cockroach

The cockroach hides until the light
Has darkened into gloomy night,
And then it scurries all around,
And eats whatever can be found:
    A drip of grease,
    A drop of fat,
    A bit of this,
    A bite of that,
And when the darkness slips away,
It hurries home and sleeps all day.

Mole

The mole doesn't hunt in the open,
Running about in the light,
He tunnels roadways under the grass,
Down where it's always night,
And there in the dark and the silence,
With no moon, no star, no sound,
He feasts on the spiders and worms and grubs
That live with the mole underground.

Elephant

The elephant,
　　So huge and fat,
Eats only *leaves*—
　　Imagine that!
You'd think that he
　　Would have to eat,
Day after day,
　　A ton of meat,
And cakes and pies,
　　And stuff like that,
To grow so big
　　And get so fat.

Frog

The frog is fond
  Of a fat young fly;
He snaps it up
  As it buzzes by,
Then gulps it down,
  With a cheerful smack,
And that's what he calls
  A nice little snack.
For the frog likes food,
  And so do I,
But I'd rather go hungry
  Than eat a fly.

Raccoon

The ring-tailed raccoons
   In their burglar masks,
Come to the cornfield,
   Unwelcome, unasked,
And pick the corn
   In the dead of night,
Husking the ears
   By the moon's pale light.
They wolf it down
   Too fast to taste,
Gobbling and gulping
   In greedy haste,
Stuffing themselves
   Till just before day
When, silent as thieves,
   They sneak away.

Mosquito

She pricks with a needle so small and thin,
You never feel it sinking in,
But down it goes, piercing the skin,
For a tiny drop to drink that's fresh,
A drop that's drawn from human flesh,
And then she'll live and then she'll thrive,
For it's bright red blood that keeps her alive.

Dog

He likes to chew
On a nice, big bone,
Gnawing and scraping it
Clean as stone,
And even then
He can't let it go,
But keeps on gnawing,
Careful and slow,
Until at last
He goes off alone,
Digs a hole,
And buries the bone.

Swan

The swan on the lake loves to snack
   On the weeds that grow below,
So she sticks her head under the water,
   As far as her neck will go,
And there she cuts herself greens,
   Slashing and clipping and snipping,
Then brings them back to the surface
   All wet and bedraggled and dripping.
Now she drops them on the water
   For a lunch of the loveliest treats,
And keeps swimming along beside them,
   Floating as she eats.

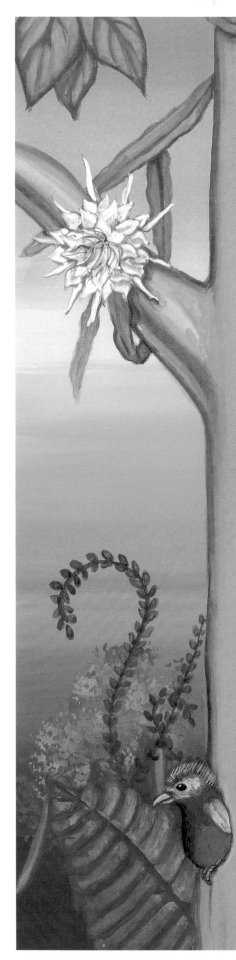

Snake

From the tip of his tail
   To the top of his nose,
The snake is as bare
   As a garden hose;
No legs, no feet,
   No wings, no claws,
Nothing except
   His joint-hinged jaws,
And even his mouth
   Seems oddly useless,
Bare inside
   (He's almost toothless)
So what he eats,
   He must swallow whole—
Mouse or bird
   Or little mole—
Choke it down,
   Gulp it complete,
Fur and eyes,
   Feathers and feet.
This will give him
   A bellyache,
Or at least it would
   If he weren't a snake.

Last Word

What creatures eat is up to them:
Their taste, their choice, their need, their whim.
And so for me—I'd rather eat
A luscious cake that's rich and sweet
Than slugs or grass or rotten meat:
 Wouldn't you?